The Palace of Stars

by Patricia Lakin ★ pictures by Kimberly Bulcken Root

TAMBOURINE BOOKS ★ NEW YORK

Printed in Hong Kong by
South China Printing Company (1988) Limited

Library of Congress Cataloging in Publication Data

Lakin, Pat. The palace of stars/by Patricia Lakin;
illustrated by Kimberly Root.—1st ed. p. cm.
Summary: After many Saturday outings at the expense of Great-uncle
Max, Amanda takes him for a surprise treat to what she calls the
palace of stars.
[1. Great-uncles—Fiction.]   I. Root, Kimberly Bulcken, ill.   II. Title.
PZ7.L1586Pal 1993 [E]—dc20 92-36796 CIP AC
ISBN 0-688-11176-9.—ISBN 0-688-11177-7 (lib. bdg.)

10 9 8 7 6 5 4 3 2 1
First edition

Amanda loved her Saturday outings at the zoo with her great-uncle Max. When he came to call, they walked arm in arm all the way to their trolley stop.

"I'm paying for two," he told the conductor, and tossed their fare into the box.

They both fed the seals, then roared with the lions,
and ended the day with ice cream.

"What flavor?" asked Uncle Max.
"It's so hard to choose."
He'd always say, "Take one of each."

Amanda hop-skipped, licking her cone.

Uncle Max tapped along with his cane.

But on one of their trips, Uncle Max changed their route to browse in the window at Stern's.

"I love that Scottie purse!"

"My treat," said Uncle Max.

Amanda swung her first purse proudly over her arm and gave Uncle Max a big hug.

Three Saturdays later Uncle Max came to call. And Amanda had planned a surprise.

"I've been saving for weeks," she told Uncle Max. "And now it's my turn to treat *you*."

She slipped on her coat and took her new purse with her red wallet inside.

They walked arm in arm past their old trolley stop. She led him across the steel tracks.

"We're not going to the zoo?" asked Uncle Max.

"I've planned something else," Amanda told him. They boarded the first trolley car.

"I'm paying for two," Amanda announced. She tossed her coins into the box.

"Where are we going?" said Uncle Max.

"A favorite place of mine."

"A joke shop?" he guessed.

"Nothing like it," she said. "It's a mansion filled with velvet and gold."

"Museum?" he guessed.

"I'll give you more clues. It's got candy and magical things. I call it the palace of stars."

He tried to think. She tugged on his cane. "Come on, Uncle Max. Here's our stop!"

They crossed the wide street and stood underneath a theater's gigantic marquee.

"Why, we're going to the movies." Uncle Max twirled his cane. "We'll see Fred Astaire and John Wayne!"

"Saturday matinee!" Amanda said. "We'll be here the whole afternoon. We'll see the cartoons and previews and news and there'll be two movies at least."

"Tickets for two," she told the cashier. Then she opened the gold door for him.

She brought Uncle Max to the long candy stand.
He pressed his nose up to the glass.
"How can I choose?"
"We could take one of each." Amanda added, "My treat."
She dumped out her coins and started to count.
But he called to her, "Nonpareils."

She gave him her hand in the huge darkened room. They felt their way down the long aisle.

"Here are good seats," Amanda said.

"Comfy." He bounced. "Candy?" He offered her some.

"Now turn around," she told Uncle Max just as the theater went black.

A white burst of light shot out of a hole. It caught dust spots that danced in its beam. Then it splashed its way up on the screen.

"Well, now," he whispered with his chin on his cane, "I've seen magic and candy and velvet and gold, but where are the stars to be found?"

Amanda leaned back and pointed way up.

Uncle Max held his breath as he stared.

The ceiling was glowing with twinkling stars and soft clouds that floated through space.

"Thanks for my Saturday matinee treat." Uncle Max placed a kiss on her hand.

And they sat arm in arm, with their heads resting close, sharing candy and watching the show.